ALL KINDS OF CASTLES

Annie M. Wyatt

This is a work of fiction. All of the characters, names, incidents, organizations, and dialogue in this novel are either the products of the author's imagination or are used fictitiously.

Archway Publishing books may be ordered through booksellers or by contacting:

Archway Publishing
1663 Liberty Drive
Bloomington, IN 47403
www.archwaypublishing.com
844-669-3957

Because of the dynamic nature of the Internet, any web addresses or links contained in this book may have changed since publication and may no longer be valid. The views expressed in this work are solely those of the author and do not necessarily reflect the views of the publisher, and the publisher hereby disclaims any responsibility for them.

Any people depicted in stock imagery provided by Getty Images are models, and such images are being used for illustrative purposes only.
Certain stock imagery © Getty Images.

ISBN: 978-1-6657-3145-4 (sc)
ISBN: 978-1-6657-3146-1 (hc)
ISBN: 978-1-6657-3147-8 (e)

Print information available on the last page.

Archway Publishing rev. date: 12/12/2022

To you,
the one curled up with a child.
I hope these pages
illuminate your imagination
and remind you that anything is possible.

Once upon a time,
A boy lived in a castle.

This castle was his home,
Among many more.
Windows and glass everywhere,
Available to enter, door by door.

As the boy explored the city,
He saw castles of every shape and size.
As he walked the streets,
Each new castle was like a surprise.

Usually they were square,
At times rectangle.
It was the ones with the balconies he loved,
Because the plants would dangle.

Sometimes the boy would leave the city,
Off to the country he would go.
He was guaranteed to see new castles,
But these usually more low.

Out in these meadows,
The boy would discover,
Castles for donkeys, goats, and sheep,
Castle barns, one after the other.

Then stood out a special castle,
Or a barn as they say.
This was his favorite,
Do you know what gave it away?

Inside was the horse,
Regal and tall,
With a mane made of gold,
And plenty of hay in his stall.

This wasn't the fanciest castle,
The boy had ever seen,
But he knew it was magical,
And always pristine.

The boy continued on his path,
Exploring even more.
He was hoping one day,
To see castles on the shore.

But what he ran into next,
Was a castle smaller than all.
It was for a reptile,
One that wasn't too tall.

This was the home of the turtle,
The one that wanders along.
His castle just a shell,
Yet beautiful and strong.

The boy began to ponder,
It seems castles are everywhere.
Can anyone have a castle?
Is that really fair?

Of course, it made sense,
It all became so clear.
Castles are homes wherever you live,
With those you love most dear.

The boy headed back to his city,
To his castle in the sky,
With a smile to himself,
And he knew why.

It's a castle for you,
And a castle for me.
Home is where the heart is,
That is the key.

Acknowledgment:

To my home, Kyle, Winston, Arthur and
George. You are my inspiration.
To my Mom and Dad, for putting books on
my shelf and dreams in my heart.
I love you all dearly.

CPSIA information can be obtained
at www.ICGtesting.com
Printed in the USA
BVHW011454040423
661730BV00006B/277